Copyright © 1997 by Nord-Süd Verlag AG, Gossau Zürich, Switzerland
First published in Switzerland under the title *Kleiner Dodo lass den Drachen fliegen!*
English translation copyright © 1997 by North-South Books Inc.

All rights reserved.
No part of this book may be reproduced or utilized in any form
or by any means, electronic or mechanical, including photocopying,
recording, or any information storage and retrieval system,
without permission in writing from the publisher.

First published in the United States, Great Britain, Canada,
Australia, and New Zealand in 1997 by North-South Books,
an imprint of Nord-Süd Verlag AG, Gossau Zürich, Switzerland.

Distributed in the United States by North-South Books Inc., New York.

Library of Congress Cataloging-in-Publication Data is available.
A CIP catalogue record for this book is available from The British Library.
ISBN 1-55858-786-1 (trade binding)
1 3 5 7 9 TB 10 8 6 4 2
ISBN 1-55858-787-X (library binding)
1 3 5 7 9 LB 10 8 6 4 2
Printed in Belgium

For more information about our books, and the authors and artists
who create them, visit our web site: http://www.northsouth.com

Serena Romanelli

LITTLE BOBO
SAVES THE DAY

Illustrated by Hans de Beer

NORTH-SOUTH BOOKS

NEW YORK / LONDON

Bobo the little orangutan lived deep in the jungle. He loved swinging from tree to tree, having races with his friends. But most of all he loved his violin, and he took it with him wherever he went. It was his most prized possession—a gift from his uncle Darwin.

Uncle Darwin lived far away, beside a lake, between the green mountains. His cave was crammed with strange objects, which Uncle Darwin had brought back from his many travels.

Uncle Darwin was always pleased when Bobo came to visit him, and he always had time to play with Bobo, to make things with him, or to tell him stories.

On one visit Bobo and Uncle Darwin decided to make a kite. First they went to the lake and cut some reeds to make a frame. Then they went into the cave to look for paper and string. In the cave Bobo found a little flute.

"You can have it if you want," said Uncle Darwin.

"Oh, thank you," said Bobo.

They worked all day, until at last the kite was finished. It was as big as an eagle, as light as a leaf, white like the clouds, and all ready to fly.

Bobo and Uncle Darwin were pleased with their handiwork. But they
had worked up quite an appetite, so they set the kite aside and sat down
to eat. Uncle Darwin handed Bobo something hard and clear that had
fruit juice in it.

"What is this? I've never seen anything like it," said Bobo.

"That's a glass. I just found it. Humans drink out of them. Have you
ever seen a human, Bobo?" asked Uncle Darwin. "Keep away from them!
If they catch you, they'll make you into soup. Or they'll stuff you."

"How horrible! How would I recognize a human?" asked Bobo.

"Oh, that's easy. They have only two hands. Now, go and get your
violin," said Uncle Darwin as he stretched out in the hammock. "I'd like
to hear you make some music."

Bobo began to play the special tune his uncle liked best.

Suddenly Uncle Darwin sat up. He staggered out of the hammock and groaned.

"Uncle, what's the matter? Don't you like my music?"

"I do, Bobo. I really do. But I've got such a stomachache." Uncle Darwin groaned again.

Bobo jumped up. "Oh, no! Isn't there anything that will help?"

"Only medicine would help, and only humans have medicine. Don't worry, Bobo, the pain will go away eventually. Let's go to bed."

But Bobo couldn't sleep. Next to him Uncle Darwin tossed and turned in bed, groaning.

"Poor Uncle, he is so sick," thought Bobo. "I'll go and find that medicine. I'm not afraid of humans! After all, they've got only two hands!"

Bobo quietly crept out of the cave.

Bobo swung through the jungle from tree to tree. It was very dark. Strange noises and eerie cries came from all sides.

"I'm not afraid! I'm not afraid!" Bobo kept telling himself. Then something big swished past and brushed against Bobo's nose. Bobo panicked and started running. Soon he was completely lost. He had no idea which way to go in the dark.

"Oh, Uncle Darwin, I really wanted to help you," Bobo whispered sadly. "Now I'll have to wait until it gets light to find my way again." He climbed up to a thick branch and fell asleep, exhausted.

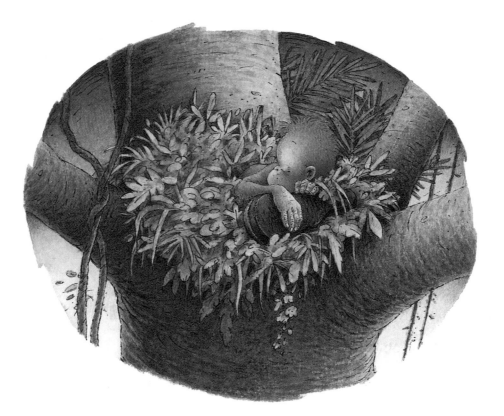

Day slowly dawned. Bobo woke up and looked around him, confused. "Oh yes, the medicine! I've got to get medicine for Uncle Darwin," he said. He peered through the branches. In the morning light everything looked friendly. He swung quickly down the tree. And there he saw . . . a creature with two hands! A human!

Shocked, Bobo let go of the branch, and landed with a thump.

The little human cried out in alarm, and he and Bobo stared at each other nervously.

"Please don't stuff me, oh please! Please don't make me into soup!" cried Bobo. "I've got to help my uncle."

"Who? What? Me?" asked the little human. Then he laughed. "What funny ideas! My name is Pico. What's yours?"

Bobo laughed too, with relief. "I'm Bobo," he said. Then he explained why he was lost in the jungle. "Are you lost too?" he asked Pico.

"No, I'm not lost. I just came here to paint. But I dropped everything because you gave me such a shock."

Bobo looked at the ground. With his four hands he picked up the tubes of paint in a flash.

"I like to come here very early to try to paint the shades of dawn. They're so pretty," said Pico, sorting his paintbrushes.

"I like to play my violin early in the morning," said Bobo. He took his violin out and began to play Uncle Darwin's special tune. Suddenly he broke off.

"That's super," said Pico. "Don't stop."

Bobo looked sad. "That tune reminds me of my uncle Darwin. He is sick with a pain in his stomach. He needs medicine, Pico. Do you know where I can find some medicine for him?"

"Come with me. We've got lots of medicine at home."

"But will your parents make me into soup?"

"Stop it! That's just silly. Come on now, don't be scared," said Pico, leading the way.

Silent as a shadow, Bobo followed his new friend. All was quiet. The village was still asleep. The only sound was Bobo's heart thumping.

"Come inside with me," whispered Pico.

But Bobo said he preferred to stay outside. "It's not that I'm scared, Pico. Oh, no. I'm not scared at all," he muttered. But he really wanted to run away!

Bobo waited impatiently. Soon Pico returned and handed Bobo a bottle of medicine. Bobo put it carefully in his violin case. He took out the little flute and gave it to Pico. "Thanks for your help," he said. "Now you can make music too."

"That's super!" said Pico, beaming with pleasure. "And here's a paintbrush and some paints for you. Now you can paint pictures too. Will you come back and visit me?"

"Yes, Pico. Sometime soon."

Bobo hurried back to Uncle Darwin. He rushed into the bedroom and handed him the medicine.

"Are you crazy? You've been among humans!" Uncle Darwin shouted, horrified. But he quickly calmed down, relieved that Bobo had returned safely. "Ah, that's doing me good!" he said as he slowly sipped the medicine. Before long he sat up and smiled. "I think it's time to fly our kite."

"Great!" said Bobo happily. "But wait. I have a surprise for you. Close your eyes."

After a while Bobo told Uncle Darwin to open his eyes. There was the kite. But it was no longer white.

"How did you do that?" exclaimed Uncle Darwin. "It's beautiful!"

"Yes, it's super, isn't it?" said Bobo with a smile. He told Uncle Darwin all about his adventures and his new friend Pico.

Then they went outside and flew the kite for hours and hours.

Uncle Darwin and Bobo were proud of their wonderful paper bird that soared above the treetops, bigger and brighter than all the birds in the jungle.